George Brown,
CLASS CLOWN
Dribble, Dribble, Drool!
FIGHTING

For Ian, who loves shooting hoops—NK

For Mom and Dad—AB

GROSSET & DUNLAP
Penguin Young Readers Group
An Imprint of Penguin Random House LLC

Library of Congress Cataloging-in-Publication Data is available.

ISBN 9780448482866 10 9 8 7 6 5 4 3 2 1

George Brown, Class Clown

Dribble, Dribble, Drool!

by Nancy Krulik

illustrated by Aaron Blecha

Grosset & Dunlap

An Imprint of Penguin Random House

FIGHTING
FERRETS

"Pass it!" Julianna shouted as George Brown dribbled the basketball down the court. "I'm open!"

But George didn't pass the ball. He just kept dribbling down the court. Finally, he stopped near the basket . . . aimed . . . and shot!

The basketball **soared** through the air.

It bounced off the backboard with a thud.

It swirled around and around the rim.

It teetered. It tottered.

And then . . .

Plop. The ball fell to the ground without going through the hoop.

"Oh man!" George groaned. "I was sure I was gonna **sink that one**."

"That's what you get for being a ball-hog," Julianna told him.

"Why didn't you pass?" Coach Hooper asked George. "Julianna had a **clear shot**."

George shrugged. "I wanted to be the one to score," he replied.

"It doesn't matter which player scores," Coach Hooper told him.

"Remember, there is no *i* in *team*." George rolled his eyes. Coach Hooper said that same thing **every practice**.

"I think you could all use some more shooting practice," Coach Hooper told the team. "Our first game is Saturday afternoon. I want the Fighting Ferrets to come out on top."

"How about a game of horse?" Julianna asked the coach. "That's a really **fun way** to practice shooting."

George groaned. He hated playing horse. The whole point of the game was for every player to make the exact same shot the first player had made. That was no problem for Julianna. She was one of the **best players** in the Beaver Brook Junior Basketball League and could make any kind of shot—a layup, a free throw, even a jump shot.

But George wasn't as sure of a shot as

Julianna. And every time he missed the basket, he got another letter in the word *horse*. George always felt **rotten** when he missed that fifth shot and got the letter *e*, because that meant he was out.

"Why don't you **go first**, Julianna?" Coach Hooper passed her the ball.

"Sure thing, Coach!" Julianna **dribbled** the ball three times as she ran toward the basket. Then she grabbed it with two hands and took her shot.

The ball banked off the backboard, and fell right through the net.

"Nice shot!" Coach Hooper exclaimed excitedly. "Now it's your turn, Alex. See if you can copy **exactly** what Julianna just did."

Alex grabbed the ball and dribbled three times as he ran toward the basket. Then he grabbed it with two hands and . . .

George couldn't watch anymore. Not because he was worried his best friend might miss the shot. George couldn't watch because he was too worried about what was going on **inside his belly** to think about anything else.

There were bubbles dribbling around inside of George. Hundreds of them.

They were bouncing up and down and all around.

Gulp. That could only mean one thing. The **magical super burp** was back. And that was *ba-a-ad*! Because whenever the burp appeared, it brought trouble.

The bubble trouble had all started when George and his family first moved to Beaver Brook. George's dad was in the army, so the family moved around a lot. George had had plenty of experience at being the new kid in school. So he'd expected the first day in his new school to **stink**. First days always did. But *this* first day was the stinkiest.

In his old school, George had been the class clown. He was always **pulling pranks and making jokes**. But George had promised himself that things were going to be different at Edith B. Sugarman Elementary School. No more pranks. No more **squishing red Jell-O** between his teeth and telling everyone it was blood. No more trouble.

Unfortunately, being the well-behaved kid in a new school also meant that George was the new kid with **no new friends**. No one at Edith B. Sugarman Elementary School even seemed to notice him. It was like he was invisible.

That night, George's parents took him to Ernie's Ice Cream Emporium just to cheer him up. While they were sitting outside and George was finishing his root beer float, a **shooting star** flashed across the sky. So George made a wish.

I want to make kids laugh—but not get into trouble.

Unfortunately, the star was gone before George could finish the wish. So only half came true—the first half.

A minute later, George had a funny feeling in his belly. It was like there were hundreds of **tiny bubbles** bouncing around in there. The bubbles hopped up and down and all around. They ping-ponged their way into his chest, and bing-bonged their way up into his throat. And then . . .

George let out a big burp. A *huge* burp. A SUPER burp!

The super burp was **loud**, and it was *magic.*

Suddenly George lost control of his arms and legs. It was like they had minds of their own. His hands grabbed straws and **stuck them up his nose** like a walrus. His feet jumped up on the table

and started dancing the hokey pokey. Everyone at Ernie's Emporium started laughing. The laughing sounded great—just like the old days. Unfortunately, the sound of his parents **yelling** at him for misbehaving *also* sounded a whole lot like the old days.

The magical super burp came back lots of times after that. And every time it did, George got **in trouble**.

Bing-bong. Right now, the bubbles were beating on his bladder and leaping over his lungs.

Ping-pong. The bubbles trampled their way onto George's tongue.

Gling-glong. They gathered around his gums.

And then . . .

Bubble bubble. George was in trouble.

"Dude, no!" Alex shouted.

Dude, *yes*! The magical super burp was on the loose. Whatever the burp wanted to do, George *had* to do. And right now, what the burp wanted to do was **play horse**.

But not the basketball kind of horse. The next thing George knew, he was galloping around the court. Like a *real* horse.

"George! What are you doing?" Coach Hooper shouted. "Get back in line. You have to **wait your turn**."

Magical super burps don't like waiting. They like playing. And *neighing*.

"Neigh! Neigh!" George shouted.

"George, cut it out," Julianna insisted. "You're **ruining** the game."

"Neigh! Neigh!" George shouted again. He galloped faster and faster around the court like a wild horse on the prairie.

Some of the other kids on the team started to **laugh**. They thought George was hilarious.

But Coach Hooper sure didn't.

"George, basketball is **serious business**," he said. "Practice is over in ten minutes. And we haven't worked on dribbling yet."

That was all the burp had to hear! The next thing George knew, he was **galloping** across the court at top speed. His feet stopped right in front of Coach Hooper.

George looked up, opened his mouth, and then . . . he let a big dribble of **ooey gooey spit** drool out of his mouth. The spit ran over his lips, down his chin, and *right onto Coach Hooper's brand-new white high-tops*!

"That's what I call dribbling!" said a tall, skinny kid named Nick, laughing.

George opened his mouth a little wider and dribbled out a **longer string** of ooey gooey drool. He dribbled. And dribbled. And . . .

Pop! Just then, George felt something **burst** in the bottom of his belly. Then all the air rushed out of him. The magical super burp was gone!

But George was still there, with a **glob of drool** on his chin.

"What do you have to say for yourself?" Coach Hooper asked him.

George opened his mouth to say, "I'm sorry." And that's exactly what came out.

Coach Hooper took a deep breath. "George, I think you're done for the day. You better **go home** now."

George didn't argue. It was better to leave before Coach got any angrier.

"Yes, sir," he said.

George turned and headed for the door. What a rotten practice. This day couldn't get any worse.

Or could it?

Just as George reached the door to the gym, he saw something **really horrible**. Someone he disliked almost as much as he hated the magical super burp.

Louie Farley.

George wondered how long he'd been standing there.

"I feel sorry for your team," Louie said as George walked toward him. "They won't win any games with a **loser** like you around."

George frowned. Obviously, Louie had been there long enough to see everything.

"The Fighting Ferrets are winners," George insisted. "We're going to **pulverize** you Legal Eagles when we play you."

"You wanna bet?" Louie asked him.

"Sure," George replied.

"Great," Louie said with grin. "Let's make it a bet for something *really* good."

George gulped. Louie was rich. He could afford to bet for something good. But George didn't have **a lot of money**—all he had was his allowance and the cash he made by working at Mr. Furstman's pet shop on Saturday mornings.

"How about the loser has to be the winner's butler for an **entire week**?" Louie suggested.

Phew. Louie wasn't betting anything that cost money. That was a **relief**.

"Okay," George said. "It's a bet."

"Great!" Louie exclaimed. "We play you guys a week from Sunday. And you're not just **gonna lose**. You're gonna lose so bad, you'll scream for mercy!"

$E=mc^2$
SKATE
TOILETMAN
POP

"You mean you don't know what a **butler** is, but you bet anyway?" Alex asked George later that day while the boys were talking on the phone. "Are you nuts?"

George gulped. "Is a butler **something bad**?" he asked nervously.

"Only if you lose," Alex told him. "A butler is a guy who does whatever his boss asks him to do. If you lose, Louie can make you do **whatever he wants**."

George gulped. "Oh man," he groaned.

"I should have known Louie would come up with something **really mean**. We really gotta beat the Eagles. Having to be Louie's *but*ler would be a real pain in *my* butt!"

"No kidding," Alex agreed. "We'll work **extra hard** at practice this week so that doesn't happen."

"Thanks," George said.

"Listen, I gotta go," Alex said. "I still have to finish the social studies homework for tomorrow. And then I have to polish the buckle on my **school safety monitor** belt."

George didn't understand why Alex wanted to be a school safety monitor. Behaving in school was a hard enough job. Making sure everyone *else* behaved had to be even harder.

"You really like being a safety monitor?" George asked his best friend.

"The safety patrol is important," Alex told him. "We make sure everybody follows the rules."

"Rules are a **pain in the neck**," George muttered.

"Maybe," Alex said. "But imagine what would happen if we didn't have any."

Actually, that didn't seem **so bad** to George. But he didn't say that. Instead he said, "I gotta get on that social studies assignment, too. I'll see you tomorrow."

"See ya," Alex said.

As soon as he hung up the phone, George turned on his computer and got ready to do his homework. But before he could start, he spotted an **invitation** from Louie in his e-mail. That was strange. Louie usually didn't invite George to anything—unless Louie's mother made him.

George looked more closely at the e-mail. It was an invitation to a **special edition** of a *Life with Louie* webcast. And Louie had sent it out to everyone in the whole school. Now it made sense. Louie wanted everyone to watch his **dopey show**. Being the center of attention was what he did best.

The webcasts were usually pretty dumb. But George figured watching Louie **make a fool of himself** was better than social studies. So he clicked the link.

And a moment later, there was Louie. His webcast had already started.

"And then he drooled all over his coach's sneakers . . ."

George couldn't **believe** his ears. Louie was broadcasting a special edition of *Life with Louie* just so he could make fun of George.

What kind of jerk would do something like that?

A Louie Farley kind of jerk. That's what kind.

"I feel bad for the Ferrets," Louie continued. "With a **super loser** like George on their team, they're never gonna win games. I am predicting right now that my team, the Legal Eagles, will be the Beaver Brook Junior Basketball League champs this year."

George clicked off his computer and **buried his head** in his hands. By now everyone was probably laughing about George Brown, Town Loser.

Nothing could cheer George up. Except maybe a handful of his mom's homemade **chocolate-chip cookies**. So George got up and headed into the kitchen.

"Hello there, soldier," George's dad

greeted him. He was sitting at the kitchen table, looking at **some kind of book**.

"Hi," George said sadly.

"What's wrong?" his dad asked him.

"Nothing," George answered. There really wasn't anything else he could say. George had never told his parents about the **problems** the super burp caused him. They probably wouldn't have believed him even if he did. George wouldn't have believed there was such a thing as a super burp, either—if it didn't keep getting him in trouble.

Alex was the only other person who knew about the burp. George hadn't even told him about it. Alex was just so smart that he had figured it out. And he'd promised to **keep it secret**.

"What are you looking at?" George asked his dad. He was trying to change the subject.

“A photo album,” his dad answered. “I’m looking at **pictures of me** when I played junior league basketball.”

“You were on a basketball team?” George asked, surprised.

“Yep,” his dad replied. “I was just a year **older** than you are now. Here, take a look. See if you can find me.”

George stared at the team picture in the photo album, trying to figure out which of the kids was his dad. Finally, he spotted a kid with short hair and ears that **stuck out like a monkey's**.

"Is that you?" he asked, pointing to the kid in the picture.

"Yup," his dad said. "I haven't changed that much, have I?"

"Well, you're taller," George said. It was so weird seeing his dad look like that. Whenever George thought of his dad as a kid, he just pictured him with a big grown-up head on a **little kid body**.

"Check out this one," George's dad said, turning the page. "I'm making a jump shot."

George started cracking up. His dad had really skinny legs with **knobby knees**. And his tongue was **hanging out** of the side of his mouth.

“Okay, so my form wasn’t that great,” his dad said with a laugh.

Looking at the photos gave George an idea. “Can I borrow **your camera**?” he asked his dad. “I want to take pictures of my team at the next practice.”

“Sure,” his dad said. “You never know. Maybe someday you’ll want to show *your* kid what you looked like when you played in the junior basketball league.”

George didn’t know what to say to that. It was **hard to imagine** himself as a grown-up dad. In fact, whenever he tried, all he could picture was his fourth-grade-size **kid head** on a big grown-up body.

Now *that* was weird.

But not as weird as being a fourth-grade-size kid with a giant super burp **following him around** everywhere he went.

George sure wished he could get rid of that burp. And soon. Because if the super burp got him in any more trouble like it had today, there would be **plenty** of pictures of fourth-grade George around—on wanted posters.

And every poster would say the same thing: BEWARE OF BURPER.

12

Chapter 3

"Your shoe is untied," Alex told a fifth-grader named Casey. "That's a **safety hazard**."

George stood on the side of the playground on Monday morning, watching as his best friend spoke to the older boy.

"Thanks for telling me," Casey said.

He bent down and began to tie his shoelace.

"You can't bend over like that in the middle of a **crowded playground**," Alex told him. "Someone might trip over you. Tripping people is against the rules!"

"How am I supposed to tie my shoe if I don't bend down?" Casey asked him.

"Alex is really going crazy with this safety monitor thing," George said to Sage, Chris, and Julianna. "I think he's **memorized** every school rule there is."

"What's he writing in that notebook?" Sage wondered.

"He's putting Casey on report," Chris answered.

"On *what*?" Sage asked.

"Report. They do the same thing in **the army**," George explained. "My dad told me about it. It's when they tell your commanding officer that you did something wrong."

"Isn't that **tattling**?" Sage asked.

George shrugged. "Sort of," he agreed. "But I guess it's different when it's your job."

"I didn't know school safety monitors

did that," Julianna said. "No one has before."

"Alex does," Chris said.

"Take that hair **out of your mouth**," George heard Alex tell a second-grader named Charlotte. "You're not supposed to eat hair in school."

Charlotte pulled the **clump** of hair she'd been chewing out of her mouth. Then she twirled the **spit-covered curl** around her finger while Alex scribbled her name in his report notebook.

"I didn't know that was a school rule," Julianna said.

"I think you probably shouldn't **eat your hair** anywhere," George said. "Not just in school."

"Yeah," Sage agreed. "It's gross."

George pointed across the playground. "Speaking of gross," he said, **"Louie's here."**

Louie strolled up to where George was standing. His pals Mike and Max were right behind him—as usual.

"*You* shouldn't be calling *me* gross," Louie told George. "I'm not the Beaver Brook Junior Basketball League's champion *dribbler*!"

Max and Mike both started laughing.

"Get it?" Max asked George. "Dribble. Like drool. Because you **drooled** at your basketball practice."

George rolled his eyes. Then he smiled at Louie.

“Gee, Louie, that joke wasn’t half bad,” George said.

Louie **stared at him** in surprise. So did Chris, Sage, and Julianna.

“It was *all* bad,” George continued.

George’s friends began to **laugh**. So did Max and Mike—until Louie glared at them.

"Yeah, well . . . uh . . . um . . . ," Louie stammered. "You're a **weirdo freak**."

"Great comeback," George said sarcastically.

Louie shot him a cruel smile. "A weirdo freak who is about to be *my* butler," he added.

"Why would Georgie be **your butler**?" Sage asked Louie.

"Didn't he tell you?" Louie asked. "George and I bet on whose team is going to win when we play each other in basketball. The loser has to be the winner's butler for a week."

"We're not going to lose," George insisted. At least he hoped not.

Brrriinnngg. Just then the **school bell** rang. It was time to go inside.

As Louie skated off toward the building on his wheelie sneakers, George frowned. It was too bad there wasn't any school rule against being a **total jerk**. Because then Alex would definitely have someone to put on report.

There wasn't a bigger jerk in the whole school than Louie Farley.

COOL

"Georgie, Georgie, he's our man! If he can't do it, no one can!" Sage shouted as she leaped up in the air and waved her hands wildly.

George turned **beet red** and stared at his tuna hoagie. Everyone in the school cafeteria was staring at him.

"Did you like my cheer, Georgie?" Sage asked him.

George **groaned**. "Not really," he muttered under his breath.

"I'm going to come to every one of your games and **cheer for you**," Sage told George. Then she looked over at Julianna.

"And for the other Fighting Ferrets, too, of course," she added quickly.

"Why don't you cheer for a team that's gonna win?" Louie asked her. "*My* team. The Legal Eagles."

"What kind of name is that for a **basketball team**, anyway?" Julianna asked him.

"My dad's law firm is sponsoring our team," Louie explained. "They're paying for our **uniforms** and everything. So we're the Legal Eagles. We were going to be the Farley Legal Eagles. But that didn't fit on our uniforms."

"They're cool uniforms," Max said. "Really legal."

"The legalest," Mike added.

"That's not even a word," George told him. "Besides, it's not the uniforms that make the team. It's the **skill on the court**. And we've got plenty of that. Julianna scored six three-pointers during practice yesterday."

Julianna grinned. "I was kind of **on fire**, wasn't I?" she asked.

George nodded. "Oh yeah!"

"Well, my coach said I was amazing at playing offense," Louie boasted.

"You are," Mike told him. "You're the **most offensive player** in the whole junior basketball league."

George laughed so hard, pieces of **half-chewed tuna** flew out of his mouth.

"Are you out of your mind?"

Just then someone started **shouting** in the middle of the cafeteria.

George turned around. The shouter was a fifth-grader named Patrick. He was yelling at Alex—who was busy writing in his report notebook.

"The Edith B. Sugarman Rule Book clearly states that you can't wear two **different-colored socks**. It's against the dress code," Alex told him.

"What dress code?" the fifth-grader asked. "What rule book?"

"This rule book," Alex said, pulling a **small, wrinkly book** out of his back pocket. "It was written in 1907."

"That's, like, a hundred years ago," the fifth-grader said.

"A rule's a rule," Alex said. "No matter how old."

A few minutes later, Alex came over to the table with his lunch tray. He squeezed in between George and Julianna.

"Sheesh," Alex complained. "You'd think kindergartners were **above the law** or something."

"What are you talking about?" George asked him.

"That kid over there," Alex said, pointing to a little girl who was **crying** in the corner.

"The one with the pigtails?" Julianna wondered.

"The one with *uneven* pigtails," Alex answered. "You're **not allowed** to have one pigtail higher than the other. It's in the rule book I found last Friday behind the radiator in the library."

"What were you doing behind the radiator?" George asked him.

"Looking for **dust bunnies** for a science experiment I'm doing at home," Alex said. "My mom is such a neat freak, we don't have any dust. But I have plenty now. This book was **buried** under at least fifty years of dust."

George was about to ask what kind of experiment needed dust bunnies. But before he could, Julianna **shook her head** and looked angrily at Alex.

"Oh, come on," Julianna said. "You're gonna **report a kindergartner** for something that stupid?"

"Rules are rules," Alex told her. "You wouldn't believe how many school rules we never knew about before. I spent the **whole weekend** reading this book."

"But you made that little girl cry," Sage said.

Alex opened his mouth to speak, but Louie interrupted him.

"Can we get back to talking about how **great I am** at playing basketball?" Louie demanded.

George groaned. Louie really hated when the conversation was about anything other than him.

"I thought we were talking about how offensive you are," George recalled.

Julianna and Sage **giggled**.

"Actually, we were talking about how the Legal Eagles were the best team to cheer for, because we're winners," Louie boasted.

"And what are we?" Julianna demanded. **"Chopped liver?"**

"No," Louie said. "You guys are losers. Or you will be when we play you."

George shook his head. Louie was getting on his last nerve.

"You know what, Louie?" George said. "You're such a lousy basketball player that from now on, I'm gonna call you Cinderella."

Louie gave him a **strange look**. "Why would you do that?"

"Because you always run away from the ball," George answered with a chuckle.

The other kids started laughing, too. Even Max and Mike—at least until Louie threw them an **angry stare**.

"Joke all you want, George," Louie said. "But I'm gonna have the last laugh. You'll see."

THE
FERRET DEN
FIGHTIN
FERRETS
G

Click!

George pulled out his dad's camera and snapped a **quick selfie** as he walked into the gym Saturday afternoon. George had brought his camera to every practice this week. But what he really wanted were pictures of his **teammates** on game day.

Of course George couldn't take pictures *during* the game, because he would be **playing**. And it's hard to dribble, pass, and shoot a basketball with a camera in one hand. But he could take plenty before the game started.

A minute later, Alex walked in, carrying his gym bag. George turned and took a picture of him, too.

Alex blinked a few times at the **flash**. "Cut it out, dude," he said. "You're blinding me."

"Oh, sorry," George said, tucking the camera into his gym bag. "I just want to have **a lot of pictures** of our first game."

Just then, Julianna came running over, dribbling a basketball. "We're gonna win this one, I can feel it!" she told the boys.

"I sure hope so," Alex said.

"It would be great," George said. "But the game we really have to win is next week's—when we play Louie's team."

"We have to win *every* game, George," Julianna told him. "Otherwise, how are we going to be the **champions**?"

George didn't answer. There was no talking to Julianna when she got this way.

Julianna was very competitive. And she liked winning. *A lot*.

"So you can't **horse around** in the game like you did during practice, George," Julianna continued.

George looked down at the ground. He knew that his horsing around hadn't been his fault. It was **the burp's fault**. But he couldn't say that.

"I promise we're all going to stay focused," Alex assured Julianna. "No one's going to goof around during a real game."

"Great!" Julianna said happily. "I'm going to practice my **free throws**. You guys want to come?"

"In a minute," Alex told her. "I just want to show George something first."

As soon as Julianna ran off, George shook his head. "How could you promise Julianna that no one would **goof** around today? You know I can't promise that. I never know when my super burp is going to show up."

"Well, it isn't going to show up today," Alex assured him.

"How do you know?" George asked.

Alex reached into his gym bag. He pulled out a pair of **basketball shorts**. "Because you're going to be wearing these," he told George.

George took the shorts and held them up. "These things are **huge**," he said.

"Exactly," Alex replied. "I read all about it on the latest Burp No More Blog entry. Wearing tight pants **forces gas up** from your stomach and out your mouth. So to stop burping, you have to wear loose clothes."

George looked at the giant shorts.

"I don't know," George said. "None of the **other cures** from that Burp No More Blog have ever stopped the super burp."

"Trust me. This one will work," Alex said. "It makes perfect **scientific** sense."

George hoped Alex was right. But he wasn't exactly counting on it.

If there was one thing George knew for sure, it was that nothing about the super burp **made any sense**. Scientific or otherwise.

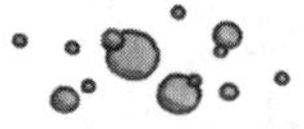

Bounce. Bounce. Bounce.

George dribbled the ball down the court toward the basket, **running** as fast as he could.

As he got closer to the basket, he heard Coach Hooper shouting at him from the sidelines. "Shoot, George! Shoot! You're clear!"

George wanted to shoot the basketball into the hoop. He really did. But he couldn't. He needed two hands to shoot. And right now he had to keep one hand on the top of his **giant shorts**. Otherwise, they were going to wind up around his ankles.

So he just stood there, **dribbling** the ball with his one free hand.

Bounce. Bounce. Bounce.

"Georgie, Georgie, he's our man!" Sage cheered from the crowd. "If he can't do it, no one can!"

George **tried not to hear her**. He just kept dribbling.

Bounce. Bounce. Bounce.

Whoosh! Just then one of the Terrifying Tigers **swooped in** and grabbed the ball right out from under George. He passed it to his teammate, who began dribbling toward the basket.

"Georgie, Georgie, he's our man!" Sage cheered again. "If he can't do it . . ."

The Tiger player **scored** a three-pointer.

"Never mind," Sage said. She plopped back down in her seat.

"George, why didn't you take your shot?" Julianna **shouted angrily** as she hurried back up the court.

George didn't answer her. He couldn't. Because if he did, he was going to give up **a lot more** than a basket. He would give up a burp! A great big *super* burp.

Ting-tong. Zing-zong. The bubbles were back. Already they had started parading onto his pancreas.

Fling-flung. Sting-stung. Some bubbles were **slipping up his spine** and ricocheting off his ribs.

George had to do something! He couldn't let the burp out now. Not in the middle of a basketball game. He had to stop it. *But how?*

George was going to have to spin those bubbles back down to his toes, like water **swirling down a drain**. It had worked before. Hopefully it would work now.

So George started **spinning** around and around.

Everything swirled and whirled inside him.

Clink-clank. Rink-rank. But the bubbles kept climbing.

Now they were tickling his trachea and **trampling onto his tongue**.

So George spun faster. And faster. *Spin. Spin. Spin.*

George was getting really, really **dizzy**. But he didn't stop. He just kept spinning and spinning and . . .

Suddenly, the bubbles started to sink back down, away from George's mouth! The bubbles slid down his throat and hopped below his heart. It was working!

"George, cut it out," Julianna said. "You're gonna make us lose!"

"George, if you don't stop, I'm going to **bench you**," Coach Hooper warned.

But George kept spinning. *Spin. Spin. Spin.*

The bubbles knocked past his knees and **kicked his calves**. They angled around his ankles and . . .

Pop! Suddenly, George felt something

burst in his belly. All the air rushed out of him. The magical super burp was gone! George had **squelched that belch**!

He raised his fists in victory.

Drop! As George's hands went up, his giant shorts went down.

There he was, standing in front of everyone in his **tighty whities**.

"George Brown, you're benched for the rest of this half!" Coach Hooper shouted.

George frowned. He'd had a feeling that was coming.

Still, it could have been **a lot worse**. Being benched beat a burp any day.

COLD
CAULIFLOWER
POPS!
MMMMM
CHRIS
MOO

"I hope you go all crazy again during Sunday's game," Louie told George during lunch on Monday afternoon. "I'm getting really tired of **tying my own sneakers**. I need a butler to do that."

"Then you better *hire* someone to do it," George told him. "Because when you're *my* butler, you'll be **so busy** carrying around my skateboard and backpack, you won't have time to tie your own shoes."

Louie laughed. "Never gonna happen," he told George. "Everyone at school heard about your **pants falling down** in the middle of last weekend's game."

"So what?" George asked him. "We still won, didn't we?"

"Yeah, but the Tigers don't have *me* on their team," Louie said. "I'm a Farley. And Farleys never lose."

"Except for that one time George beat you at **thumb wrestling**," Max reminded him.

"And that other time when George won the chance to lead the Halloween parade," Mike added.

"And then—" Max began.

Louie glared at him. Max shut his mouth, quick.

"None of that matters, because I'm a **basketball superstar**!" Louie exclaimed. "I can win all by myself. I don't even need the rest of the team."

George groaned. Louie wasn't a star. He was more like a **black hole**. A black hole that sucked the fun out of everything.

George turned his attention away from Louie and watched as Alex pulled out his **notebook** and began to put a second-grader's name in his on-report notebook.

George shook his head. "Alex is getting a little **rule-crazy** these days," he said.

"Ya think?" Julianna said **sarcastically**. "He's the most feared person in the whole school. And that includes Principal McKeon!"

"Yeah, well, I'm the most feared person on the basketball court," Louie said, bringing the conversation back to himself—as usual.

Before Louie could **brag** some more, Sage plopped her tray down on the table and squeezed in between George and Julianna. She shot George a goofy smile.

"I'm happy the Ferrets won the game last Saturday, Georgie," she said. "It was so **smart of you** to psych the other team out like that."

Louie gave Sage a funny look. So did George. He had no idea what she was talking about.

"Who else but Georgie would drop his shorts just to **make the other team laugh**?" Sage continued. "They couldn't play at all after that."

George felt his face turn red.

Dropping his shorts had been really **embarrassing**.

"Well, he won't be able to psych *me* out," Louie told Sage. "Farleys can't be psyched out."

"Yeah," Max said. "Farleys are never the psychees."

"Exactly," Mike agreed. "Farleys are always **the psychos** . . ." He stopped for a minute. "No. That can't be right."

George laughed so hard, he **snorted**.

Chris elbowed him in the side. "Don't snort. Alex told some third-grader that there's a **rule against snorting** in school."

"And you definitely don't want to be put on report," Julianna said. "I heard that Principal McKeon is making everyone who is on report stay after school this afternoon to paint the playground equipment. That would mean missing basketball practice."

George knew what Julianna meant. Coach Hooper had his *own* rules. And one of the rules was that anyone who **missed a practice** had to sit on the bench during the next game.

"Well, I'm getting myself another slice of pizza," Louie said. "Our team's got practice this afternoon, too. And I'm going to need a **lot of energy** to score all those points."

"You better hurry," Max told him.

"Pizza goes fast around here."

"Don't worry about me," Louie replied. "I'm faster than anyone."

Louie reached down and popped the wheels out of the bottom of his **wheelie sneakers**. Then he jumped up and started roller-skating across the cafeteria.

Louie skated on one foot.

He skated on the other foot.

He turned around and **skated backward**.

And then . . .

Bam! Louie skated right into Alex.

Slam! Alex landed right on his **rear end**.

Wham! Louie fell on top of Alex.

"That's it!" Alex shouted angrily from **underneath a pile** of Louie. "You're on report."

"No way!" Louie told him. "They

didn't even *have* wheelie sneakers back when that rule book was written. So there can't be a rule against them."

"No, but there is a rule about walking backward," Alex told him. "And about **tackling someone**. So you're on report *twice*."

Louie stared at Alex in disbelief. "You can't put me on report!" he insisted. "Farleys don't go on report."

"Now they do," Alex told him.

As Alex started writing **Louie's name** in his notebook, George and Chris walked past them on their way to the playground.

"Guess you won't be going to your team practice today," George said to Louie as he passed by.

Louie shot him an angry look.

George smiled back at him. "Just so you know," he said. "I like my shoelaces **double-knotted**."

Chapter 7

"There is *no* way I am missing practice to **paint playground equipment**," Louie growled as he stormed onto the playground with Max and Mike a few minutes after George and Chris. "I need to work on my layups. And besides, Farleys don't paint."

"You're gonna paint," George told him. "Just like **everyone else** who was put on report."

"I'm not like everyone else," Louie said.

George laughed. He couldn't argue with that. There was no one quite like Louie.

"It's too bad this didn't happen next week," Louie said with **a frown**. "Then I could have had my butler take the punishment for me." He smiled pointedly at George.

"Not gonna happen," George said. "I'm not going to lose this bet."

Louie thought for a minute. "I don't have to wait to get a butler," he said happily. "I'm rich. I'll just **pay someone** to take my punishment for me."

"You can't do that," Chris said.

"There isn't anything a Farley can't do," Louie told him. He turned to Max and Mike. "Which one of you guys wants to earn some cash and **take my punishment**?"

"I'll do it," Max told Louie.

"No way," Mike said. "I'll do it. I'm a great painter."

"Oh yeah?" Max asked him. "What have you ever painted?"

George turned to Chris. "I don't feel like spending **my recess** listening to this," he said. "You want to go see what Julianna's doing?"

"Definitely," Chris agreed. "I think she said something about **playing four-square** during recess today."

"Four-square is cool," George said. "Who else is playing?"

"I don't know," Chris told him. "But I know who *isn't* playing." He pointed to a nearby oak tree. Alex was standing there, with his notebook in hand.

"Your shirt is **buttoned wrong**," George heard Alex say. "That's against the dress code. I'm putting you on report."

"I'll fix it," the second-grader said.

"Too late," Alex told him. "You're already in the book."

George shook his head. "Alex's **report list** must be ten pages long by now," he told Chris.

"We're lucky he hasn't done it to us," Chris said.

"We're his **best friends**," George told him. "No guy would *ever* put his best friends on report."

"That's true," Chris agreed.

"Hey, you guys, we have two open squares," Julianna called to Chris and George. "Come on. Let's play."

George looked at the four-square court. Sage was holding a **big red ball** and standing in the first square. Julianna was in the second square.

Ordinarily George wouldn't have wanted to hang out with Sage at recess. But he had **no choice**. You need four kids to play four-square. And Alex was busy being a safety monitor. Sage was going to have to do.

"Come on, Georgie," Sage said. She did that **weird** blinking-her-eyelashes-up-and-down thing again.

George rolled his eyes. He hated when Sage called him Georgie.

"Just serve the ball," he said as he stepped into the third square, and Chris took his place in the fourth.

"Whatever you say, Georgie." Sage **bounced the ball** once in her square and then hit it into Julianna's square.

Julianna let the ball bounce and then hit it into Chris's square.

Chris let the ball bounce and then **hit it back** to Sage.

George wasn't sure where Sage hit the ball next. He wasn't **paying any attention** to where on the court the big red ball was bouncing. He couldn't. He was too busy focusing on the bouncing that was going on inside his stomach.

There were bubbles in there. Hundreds of them. And they were all on the move!

Ding-doing. Already the bubbles were **clip-clopping** their way through his colon and inching up through his intestines.

The bubbles leaped over his larynx. They **tickled** his tonsils.

George shut his mouth, tight. He couldn't let the burp escape.

But the bubbles kept coming. They gathered on his gums. And twisted around his teeth. And then . . .

Uh-oh. The magical super burp was in charge now. George had to do whatever it wanted to do. And what the burp wanted to do was **bounce**!

The next thing George knew, he was bouncing up and down like a brown-haired, brown-eyed, **burping pogo stick**.

Bounce. Bounce. Bounce.

George bounced right out of his square.

Bounce. Bounce. Bounce.

He bounced past the **big oak tree** and around the swings.

"George, what are you doing?" Julianna said.

Bounce. Bounce. Bounce.

George bounced his way through the line of first-graders waiting to go down the slide. The kids **scattered like ants**, trying to get out of his way.

"George, please don't bounce near the little kids," his teacher, Mrs. Kelly, called from across the playground. "You're liable to step on one of them."

George wanted to stop bouncing. He really did. But he **wasn't in charge** anymore. The burp was. And what the burp wanted to do was . . .

Stop bouncing!

George was amazed. The burp had **actually listened** to his teacher.

The next thing George knew, his feet started running. But George had no idea where he was running. All he knew was that he couldn't stop.

At least not until he reached the

huge garbage dumpster near the back of the school cafeteria.

Now George wasn't running anymore. He was *climbing*—right up the side of the **stinky, smelly dumpster**.

When he reached the top, George opened his mouth and shouted, "DIVE-BOMB!"

The next thing he knew, George was diving headfirst into a big pile of **rotting** lettuce, spoiled milk, stale bread, and last week's tuna surprise. Yuck!

"Surprise!" George shouted as he threw a handful of **smelly tuna** up in the air. "It's flying fish!"

The teachers on the playground all came running.

"George, what are you doing?" Mrs. Kelly asked him. "**Get out of there** right now."

George wanted to get out of there. He really did. Who wouldn't want to get out of a stinky, smelly dumpster?

The burp. That's who. Burps love stinky, smelly stuff.

George picked up a **handful of lettuce** and . . .

Pop! Suddenly he felt something burst in his belly. All the air rushed out of him.

The super burp was gone.

But George was still there. With **spoiled milk up his nose** and tuna surprise down his pants.

Alex came running over. He watched as George stood up and looked over the edge of the dumpster.

"Boy, am I glad to see you," George said to his **best pal**. "Can you help me climb out of this thing?"

But Alex didn't help George. Instead, he took out his notebook and began to write.

"Littering is against the rules," Alex said, pointing to the **globs of tuna surprise** George had thrown onto the ground. "I'm putting you on report."

OSCAR'S
DUMPSTER
CO.

Chapter 8

"Dude, I *had* to put you on report," Alex insisted at the end of the school day. "You broke a lot of rules."

George yanked angrily on the bottom of his **too-short T-shirt**. Principal McKeon had made him change out of his garbage-covered clothes so he wouldn't **stink up** the classroom. Now he was wearing clothing from the lost and found. Nothing he had on actually fit.

"It wasn't my fault." George looked around to make sure **no one else** was listening. Then he whispered, "It was the fault of the *you-know-what.*"

"I can't put a burp on report," Alex whispered back so only George could hear.

"But I'm not going to be able to go to practice." George wasn't whispering anymore. He was **too upset** to keep his voice down any longer. "Coach is going to put in one of the kids from the bench on Sunday. Like Paulie Wurmer. All that kid does is stand there and **pick his nose**."

"Paulie might play better than you think," Alex said. "Especially if his **allergies** aren't bad on game day."

George could feel his face getting hot. He couldn't believe Alex. "You're missing the point," George told him.

"I would never do this to *you*. I would never put my best friend on report."

"Of course you wouldn't," Alex agreed.

"Exactly," George said. "Because I'm—"

"Because you're not a safety monitor," Alex interrupted.

George was **really mad** now. Alex wasn't getting it.

"If I wind up being Louie's butler, it's gonna be *your* fault for putting me on report," George grumbled.

"Louie's on report, too," Alex reminded him. "And you know Principal McKeon isn't going to let him **pay someone** to take his punishment. So he's gonna miss *his* practice, too."

Louie walked over to where George and Alex were standing. He gave them both a big smile.

"Yeah, but it won't matter," Louie said, butting his way into their conversation. "Our coach isn't **as strict** as yours. We don't have any rules that say if you miss practice, you can't play in the game."

Rules.

Boy, did George hate that word. It made him angry just hearing Louie say it.

But George was even *more* angry with Alex. **What kind of a guy** got his best friend in trouble, anyway?

A guy who *wasn't* George's best friend anymore. **That's what kind**.

"I guess I'll see you tomorrow," Alex said as he swung his backpack over his shoulder and headed for the door.

"Not if I see you first," George muttered under his breath.

"That Alex is a **real jerk**," a fifth-grader named Will groaned as he painted the merry-go-round.

“You got that right,” Will’s friend Arnie agreed. “He put me on report for **chewing the eraser** off my pencil. What kind of a stupid rule is that?”

“He’s the worst,” Will added.

“Alex is nothing but a **snitch** with a badge,” Arnie said.

George nodded. Alex the Snitch. That pretty much said it all.

“I can’t believe Principal McKeon is letting him **get away** with this,” Will said.

"I can," Arnie replied with a groan. "She's rule-crazy, just like Alex. Man, that kid makes me so mad."

If George and Alex had still been friends, he probably would have **stood up for him**. He might have told the other kids that Alex was just doing his job.

But Alex *wasn't* George's friend anymore. So George just stayed there by the ladder that led to the top of the slide, moving his paintbrush up and down.

Just then, George spotted Louie. He was wandering around the playground with a paintbrush in his hand. But he wasn't painting. He was just **pretending to be busy**. *Typical Louie.*

Suddenly, Principal McKeon walked over to Louie. She took him by the hand and dragged him to the swing set. Then she stood there and made him work.

Ordinarily, seeing Louie get in trouble would have brought a smile to George's face. But not today. Today he was **too miserable**.

And there was only one person to blame for that: Alex the Snitch.

HOME
TIME
00:00
1
0
FF
COACH
HOOPS!
FF
G

Chapter 9

"George, I'm glad to see that you came to the game even though you're benched," Coach Hooper said as George walked into the gym on Sunday afternoon. "That shows real **team spirit**."

George frowned. Even though he'd missed the Monday practice, he'd shown up for every other practice all week. He'd hoped that would have been enough to make the coach give in and **let him play**.

But obviously George was still benched. Coach Hooper was as big a stickler for **the rules** as Alex was.

George reached into his gym bag and pulled out his dad's camera. "I figured if I couldn't play, at least I could be the team photographer," he said.

"What a great idea," Coach Hooper exclaimed. "It would be terrific to have some **action shots** to show at our team banquet."

"So it's okay if I walk around the gym during the game to take pictures?" George asked hopefully.

"I don't see why not," Coach Hooper said. "Just stay **out of the way** of the players. *And don't cause any trouble.*"

George frowned. *Trouble.* The one word every adult in town seemed to use when they were talking about him. *Stupid super burp.*

Just then, Louie Farley came **strolling** into the gym. Max and Mike followed close behind.

"I said *I'd* carry Louie's gym bag," Max said as he **yanked** at the bag's handle.

"Well, I got it first," Mike said, yanking back.

"Well, I'm gonna carry it last," Max insisted. He pulled hard on the handle.

Riiiipppp.

Just then the bag **ripped open**. Louie's gym clothes flew out and landed in a heap on the floor.

Louie spun around angrily. "What happened?" he shouted.

"Max did it," Mike said.

"Mike did it," Max said.

"**I don't care** who did it," Louie told them. "Just put my stuff back in the bag."

As Max and Mike scrambled to put Louie's shorts, shirt, and sneakers back into what was left of his gym bag, Louie looked at George and smiled.

"So glad you showed up for the game," Louie said. "Now you can start being my butler as soon as the **last whistle blows**."

"Not gonna happen," George replied. "The Ferrets are gonna destroy the Eagles."

George was trying to sound really confident. But he wasn't confident at all. Already Paulie Wurmer was busy blowing his nose into a **giant wad of used tissues** while the other kids practiced free throws. That was not a good sign.

Julianna must have seen the worried look on George's face, because she came running over.

"Don't worry," she told him. "We'll win this one. I've been practicing my three-pointers all week!"

George forced a smile to his face. "That's great," he told Julianna. "I feel a lot better now."

Except he really didn't. Especially not when he saw Paulie Wurmer trip over his shoelace and **land face-first** in a pile of used tissues.

"Hey, dude," Alex said as he walked over to where Julianna and George were talking. "How's it going?"

George didn't answer Alex. "I'm going to make sure I get a shot of some of those **three-pointers**," he told Julianna. "I'm the team photographer today."

"That's awesome!" Julianna said. "My mom and dad are out of town again. This way I'll at least be able to show them some **photos of the game**."

"It would be great if you could take

some pictures of . . . ," Alex began.

But George **didn't listen** to the rest of his sentence. He just walked away. George didn't want to hear anything Alex the Snitch had to say.

Weeeeep. Just then the referee blew his high-pitched whistle. The game was **about to begin**.

As the Legal Eagles ran onto the court, Louie stopped and shot George a mean smile.

"I want an **orange soda** to be waiting for me after we win the game," he said.

"And it better be cold."

George gulped. If his team didn't win, this was going to be **longest week** of his life.

"Don't worry, George," Julianna called over. **"We've got this."**

Weeeep! The ref blew his whistle again and tossed the basketball in the air. Julianna and the Legal Eagle's center both jumped up.

Slam. Julianna got the tip-off and **hit the ball** over toward Alex.

Phew. Julianna really was on fire. Maybe the Ferrets could win this one, after all.

"Aaaachooo!" Suddenly, Paulie Wurmer let out a huge sneeze. He wiped the **wet boogers** on his hand, and picked the inside of his nose.

George frowned. Then again, maybe not.

FERRETS
FF

Chapter 10

Click! Click! Click!

George snapped three quick shots of Julianna as she leaped up and shot the ball right **into the basket**. He couldn't believe how high Julianna could jump. It was like she had pogo sticks on the bottoms of her high-tops.

Still, the shot was only worth two points. Which meant that the Ferrets were still **two points behind** the Legal Eagles. And with only a minute left to go in the second half, that was not a good sign.

Click! Click!

George raced around to the other side of the court and **snapped a few shots** of some of his other teammates. Well, most of them, anyway. He didn't take any pictures of Alex.

Swoop! Just then, Julianna **swiped the ball away** from one of the Legal Eagles. She dribbled back down the court and stopped, right in the three-point range. She took the ball in her hands, reached up, and shot!

Smack!

The ball bounced off the backboard.

Whoosh! It slid right through the basket.

"Yes!" Julianna shouted. She leaped up into the air and **pumped her fist**.

George started jumping up and down, too. The Ferrets were leading by a point. And there were only thirty seconds left in the game. Which meant it was **only thirty**

seconds until Louie became his butler.

George started to think of all the things he could make Louie do for him. Like clean his room, or carry his books, or . . .

"It's not over yet," Louie shouted, interrupting George's thoughts. "I've got the ball now."

George gulped. Louie was **really moving** down the court. He was dribbling as hard and as fast as he possibly could.

But the clock was already **counting down** the last eight seconds.

George followed Louie around the edge of the court, his camera in hand.

Julianna charged toward Louie, trying

to steal the ball away from him.

Louie **swerved around** Julianna. He dribbled to the far corner of the court. Then he turned. And shot.

Click.

George took a photo of Louie as he shot the ball. He wanted to make sure he had a great picture of Louie **missing the basket**—and losing the game for his team.

Everyone stared at the ball as it flew through the air.

Uh-oh.

George gulped. The ball was going **right for the net**. Louie might actually sink this one.

Slam! The ball hit the backboard.

Swirl! It whirled around and around on the rim. The ball **teetered** toward the outer edge. And then . . .

Swish! The ball went right through the net.

George got a **sick feeling** in his stomach.

Buzzz! The buzzer sounded. The game was over.

"WOO-HOO!" the Legal Eagles began to cheer.

Louie cheered the loudest. "WE WON!" he shouted.

George couldn't believe it. This was a nightmare. **An absolute nightmare.** But there was nothing he could do about it.

George started walking slowly back to the bench. He figured he had better put his camera back in the case now. Louie was going to have plenty for him to do. George wasn't going to have any time to take postgame pictures.

"LEGAL EAGLES RULE!" the team shouted again.

The Legal Eagles were **still cheering**. That probably meant George had a few minutes before he had to get Louie that cold orange soda. So he started looking at the photos he'd taken during the game.

There was one of Nick scoring on a free throw.

One of Stan dribbling down the court.

One of Paulie **picking his nose**.

One of Julianna making the three-pointer.

And one of Louie taking that last game-winning shot.

Hey! Wait a minute. That doesn't look right.

Quickly, George **zoomed in** on the

photo of Louie. He wanted to see the details **close up**.

Normally, there was no way George would spend this much time looking at a photo of Louie. In fact, any other time, he would have **scrolled right past it**.

But this photo of Louie meant everything. *It meant the entire game.*

FF
FF
1
9

"That last shot was **out of bounds**!" George shouted really, really loud. "It doesn't count."

The Eagles stopped cheering.

The gym got quiet.

Everyone looked at George.

"Forget it," Louie told him. "We won the game. **You lost the bet.** And there's nothing you can do about it. Now be a good butler and get me my orange soda."

"No, *we* won," George insisted. "Look. **Your foot** was out of bounds when you took the shot."

The referee came running over. "Let me see that," he said.

George handed him the camera. He **pointed to the line** on the ground. Louie's left sneaker was clearly on the outside of the line.

"See?" George asked the ref. He pointed to the bottom of the photo, where Louie's left foot was clearly over the line. "That basket **doesn't count**."

"How do we know that shot is my last basket?" Louie said. "You could have taken that photo any time."

"Nope," George said. He scrolled back on the camera. "The picture I took right before that is **Julianna's three-pointer**. She only made one of those the whole game.

Just before you took your shot. Your *only* shot the whole second half."

Louie's face turned beet red. His eyes opened wide. He was so mad, **he couldn't speak**.

But that didn't matter. Because at just that moment, Louie's mother came racing out of the bleachers and onto the court. And *she* had plenty to say.

"Don't tell me you're not going to count my **Loo Loo Poo's** basket!" she shouted at the ref.

"It appears he was out of bounds when he shot, Mrs. Farley," the referee tried to explain to her. "It's right here in this boy's photo."

Mrs. Farley **glared** at George. "Not you again," she said. "You're always causing trouble for my Loo Loo Poo."

George choked back a laugh. *Loo Loo Poo*. That was hilarious. And it never got old.

Mrs. Farley turned back to the referee. "Since when are **referees** allowed to look at photographs to make their rulings?" she demanded.

Alex walked over carrying a **small, thin booklet** in his hands.

George frowned. Was Alex going to put him on report for taking pictures now?

"Actually, Mrs. Farley," Alex said, "there's **no rule** *against* using photos. I have a copy of the Beaver Brook Junior Basketball League rule book right here. So I guess it's up to the referee to decide whether he wants to use this picture or not."

Alex smiled at George. George smiled back at him. For once, Alex's obsession with rules might actually **come in handy**.

"Well, that settles it then," Mrs. Farley said. "Loo Loo Poo's team wins. Because no one ever rules against a Farley."

George frowned. Louie did get away with a lot of stuff. Which meant . . .

"I'm sorry, Mrs. Farley," the ref said. "But I *am* ruling against Louie. Which means the Ferrets have won the game!"

"WOOOO-HOOOOOO!" Julianna shouted. "WE WON!"

The other Ferrets began to cheer. "We've got Ferret Fever! We've got Ferret Fever!"

"**You did it, George!** You won the game for us!" Alex said. He slapped him on the back.

"It never would have happened if you didn't have that **rule book** with you," George said.

"They gave us each one of them when we **got our uniforms**," Alex said. "Didn't you read yours?"

George shook his head. "Who reads rule books?"

"*I* do," Alex said. "Sometimes rules really come in handy."

George looked over at Louie. His face was purple red. **Little beads of angry sweat** were forming on his forehead and his nose.

George grinned. *This is going to be fun.*

"Oh, butler!" George shouted over to Louie. "I've got a **few jobs** for you!"

Chapter 12

"Where's your safety monitor sash?" George asked Alex early Monday morning as the boys walked to school together.

"In my backpack," Alex said. "I'm going to **turn it in** to the office at school."

"You're not going to be a safety monitor anymore?" George asked him.

Alex shook his head. **"It's not worth it,"** he said. "Everyone in school hates me because I'm the safety monitor who follows all the rules. And I would hate myself if I was a safety monitor and I didn't follow all the rules. So it's easier to just not be a safety monitor."

"Makes sense," George said. He

grinned. "Now you have more time to hang around with Chris and me."

"And more time to help you **figure out a cure** for the you-know-what," Alex said.

George nodded. But he didn't answer Alex. He couldn't. Not while there was so much going on **down inside his belly**.

Grumble. Rumble.

George stood there waiting for the bubbles to start moving up toward his mouth.

But they didn't. In fact, there weren't any bubbles in his belly at all. George's belly was completely empty—**and hungry**. George had gotten up late and only had time for a quick glass of orange juice.

"Oh, Louie," George called out. "Be a good butler and get my **emergency chocolate bar** out of my backpack."

Louie had been following George and Alex the whole way to school. He was carrying George's backpack for him. It was one of his new **butler duties**.

George waited as Louie dug around for the chocolate bar George had shoved into his bag the night before.

"Gross," Louie said. "It's **all melted**."

"I must have left my backpack over the heater in my room again last night," George said. "That's okay. Chocolate tastes better when it's melted."

Louie handed George the chocolate bar. George opened the wrapper and took a bite of the gooey chocolate.

"Delicious!" George said. Melted chocolate **oozed out of his mouth** and down his chin. "Napkin, please," he said to his butler.

Louie mumbled something angrily to himself. Then he pulled some tissues out of his pocket.

"These will have to do." George took the tissues and **wiped his face**. He looked down. Some of the chocolate had run down his chin and onto his shirt. "I can't go to school like this," he said to Louie. **"Switch shirts with me."**

"Are you nuts?" Louie said. "Why would I want to wear a T-shirt that says 'Furstman's Pet Shop'? **I don't work there.** You do. I don't work anywhere."

"This week you work for *me*, remember?" George said.

Louie frowned. He was **fuming**. But he took off his coat and his shirt.

George did the same thing. Then the boys **switched shirts**.

Louie buttoned his coat and crossed his arms across his chest so no one could see he was wearing George's shirt.

"How long are you gonna keep this up?" Alex asked George as the boys continued walking to school.

"I don't know. A little while," George said. "But not a whole week. I **can't stand** having Louie this close to me for that long. I'll get rid of him soon."

George wished getting rid of the magical super burp could be as easy as **getting rid of Louie**. But he knew that wasn't the case. The burp had made itself at home in George's belly. And it was bound to burst out of him again.

He didn't know when.

He didn't know where.

The only thing George **knew for sure** was that when those bubbles burst out, trouble was sure to follow.

Bubble trouble. Which was the worst kind.

About the Author

Nancy Krulik is the author of more than 150 books for children and young adults, including three *New York Times* Best Sellers and the popular Katie Kazoo, Switcheroo books. She lives in New York City with her family, and many of George Brown's escapades are based on things her own kids have done. (No one delivers a good burp quite like Nancy's son, Ian!) Nancy's favorite thing to do is laugh, which comes in pretty handy when you're trying to write funny books! You can follow Nancy on Twitter: @NancyKrulik.

About the Illustrator

Aaron Blecha was raised by a school of giant squid in Wisconsin and now lives with his family by the south English seaside. He works as an artist designing funny characters and illustrating humorous books, including the one you're holding. You can enjoy more of his weird creations at www.monstersquid.com.